AN AMAZING GIRL—AN AMAZING BOOK— AND NOW AMAZING PAPER DOLLS

Grace loves stories, whether they're in books or in movies or the kind her grandmother tells. And she knows *exactly* who she wants to be. She acts out the most exciting parts of all sorts of tales—from Joan of Arc to Peter Pan.

Grace's positive message encourages pride and self-confidence in children; and now with paper dolls, children will have the opportunity to dress Grace in the costumes of her various characters, while at the same time gaining creative inspiration by role-playing themselves. Also included is a press-out theater trunk so young ingenues will have a place to store the wardrobe pieces. *Amazing Grace Paper Dolls* will provide hours of fun for children as they dress Grace and play all the roles in their own individual ways.

Published by Dial Books for Young Readers
A member of Penguin Putnam Inc.
375 Hudson Street
New York, New York 10014

Amazing Grace Paper Dolls copyright © 1998 by Dial Books for Young Readers
ISBN 0-8037-2297-4
Amazing Grace Paper Dolls based on character in *Amazing Grace*,
written by Mary Hoffman and illustrated by Caroline Binch,
first published in the United States by
Dial Books for Young Readers,
a member of Penguin Putnam Inc.

Art for paper doll costumes and accessories by Judy Lanfredi
All rights reserved
Printed in the U.S.A. on acid-free paper
First Edition
1 3 5 7 9 10 8 6 4 2

Hardcover edition of *Amazing Grace* available: ISBN 0-8037-1040-2

TRUNK INSTRUCTIONS:

With the colored side of the trunk facing you, fold the box downward along the scored lines. Put a light application of glue onto each of the four side flaps marked "X". Fold the box into its final shape, and hold the sides in position until the glue is dry.

As you dress Grace in her various costumes, cut out the appropriate labels and paste them on the trunk to show all the roles that Grace has played.

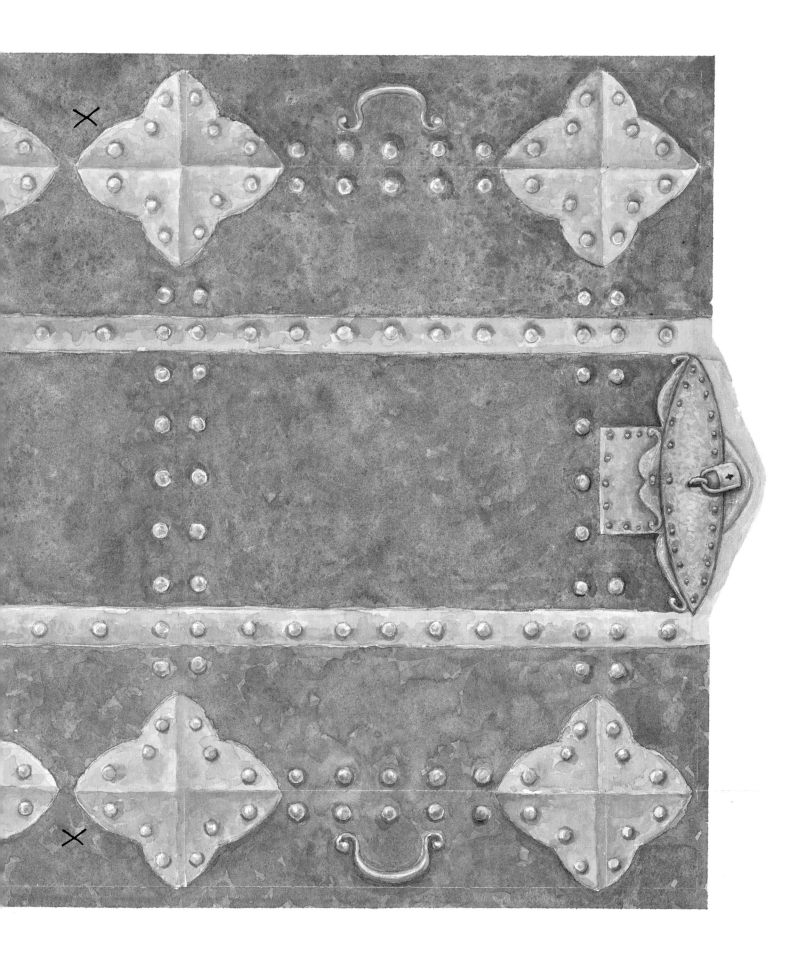

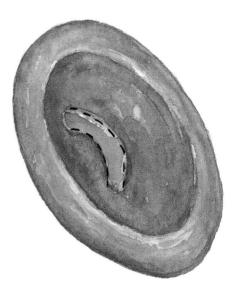

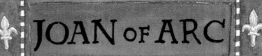

JOAN of ARC

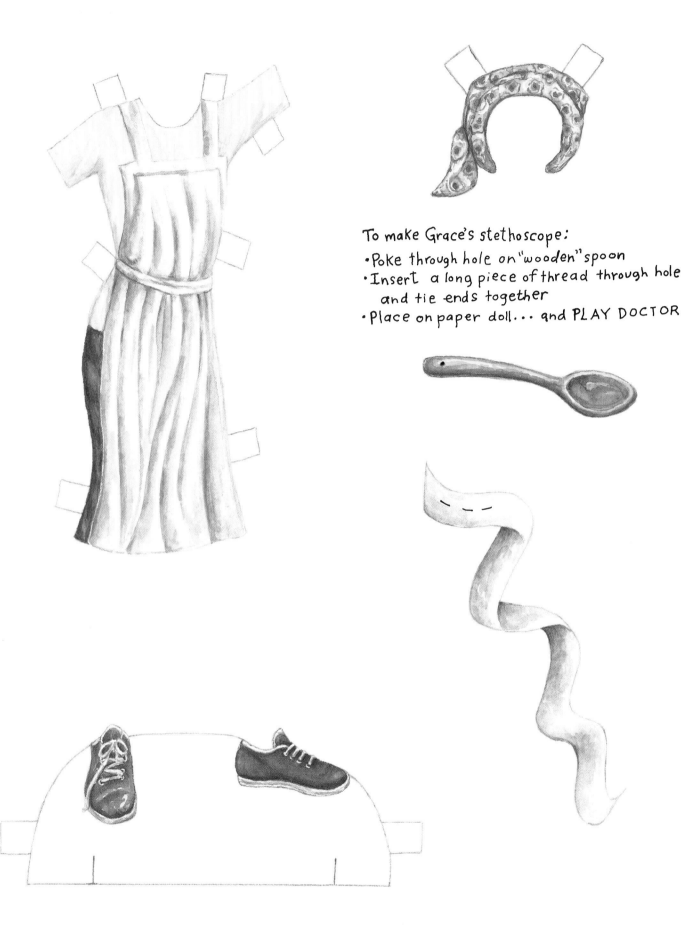

To make Grace's stethoscope:
- Poke through hole on "wooden" spoon
- Insert a long piece of thread through hole and tie ends together
- Place on paper doll... and PLAY DOCTOR

DOCTOR GRACE

ROMEO
and
JULIET

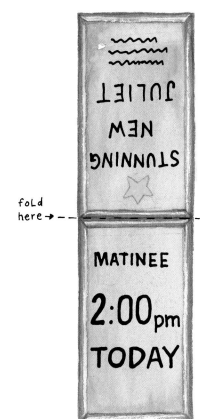

STUNNING NEW
JULIET

fold here →

MATINEE
2:00pm
TODAY

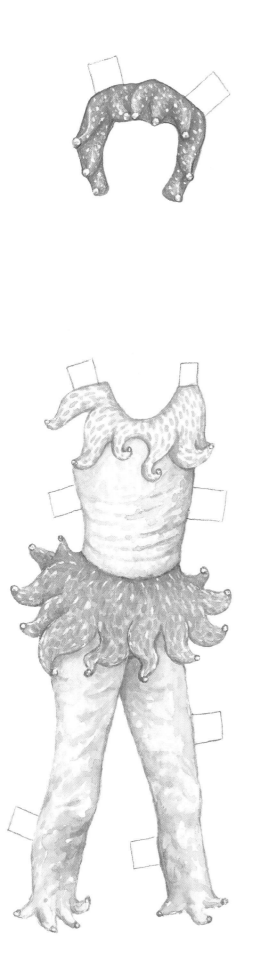

Peter Pan

SHOWBILL

Peter Pan

The Pirate

The
Adventurer

Create an Outfit for Grace!

To help you get started, we've given you a few basic shapes to work with. Do you want Grace to be a teacher, an astronaut, president, or perhaps an actress?
Be imaginative... just draw, design, and color.
Remember: Grace can be anything you want her to be!

Make your own labels for Grace's trunk!